19

 W9-AHT-217

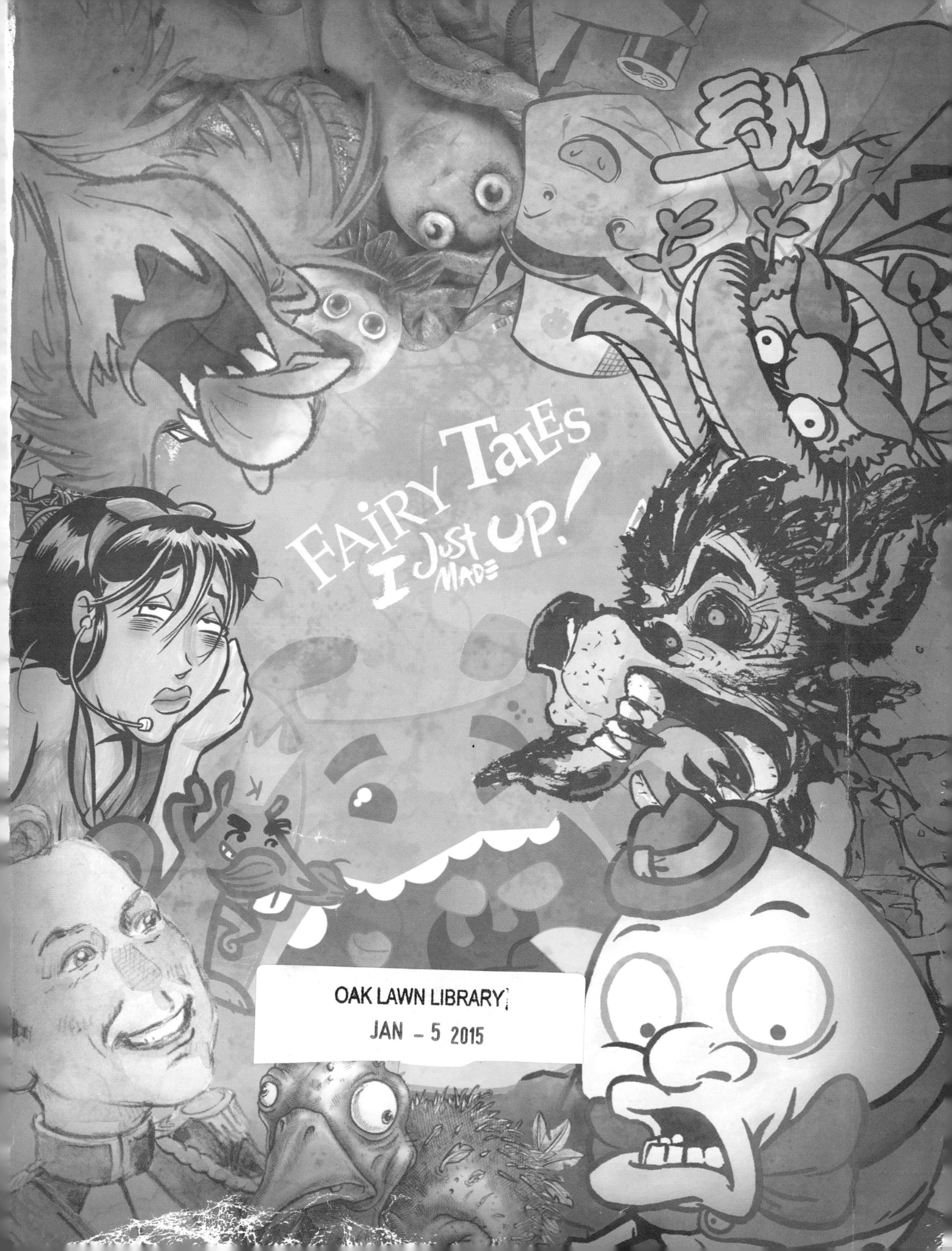
Fairy Tales I Just Made Up!

*This book is dedicated to my
wonderful partner Michelle, who
laughed at all the right bits.*

*And to the tiny human
she and I are co-creating,
who hopefully one day
will too.*

First Edition: November 2014   ISBN 978-0-9802314-4-1
© 2014 Ray Friesen. All Rights Reserved in case we need them later.
Special thanks to Burgess for his editorial powers.

W W W . F A I R Y T A L E S I J U S T M A D E U P . C O M
W W W . D O N T E A T A N Y B U G S . C O M
W W W . R A Y F R I E S E N . C O M

CONTENTS

GOLDILOX
and the
Three Dragons

Illustrated by Ray Friesen

Goldilox was called "Goldilox" because everything she touched turned to solid gold. She wasn't named after her hair color, which was more a sort of light brown anyway.

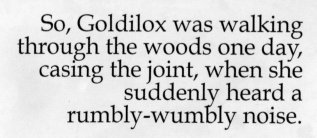

She was extremely talented at picking locks, for you see, Goldilox was a professional thief.

She had been hired by The King Of Squirrels to break into a magical tree-vault that contained the entire world's supply of acorns.

Kings love acorns.

So, Goldilox was walking through the woods one day, casing the joint, when she suddenly heard a rumbly-wumbly noise.

In a cave snoozed some dragons.

Three of them.

See? Now the title of this story makes perfect sense!

The three dragons were named SoulSmasher, ChampionCruncher, and Henry.

They were guarding the tree that contained all the acorns in the world, but they were guarding it while napping. Guarding is a really boring job.

Goldilox crept back into town, went to her local library, and checked out a book on dragononomy.

She read it all the way through, (even the pages without any pictures).

Next, she went to Ye Olde Temp Agency, and hired a Freelance Knight, who got paid by the hour.

Together, they went back into the forest, and tiptoed ever-so-quietly up to the sleeping dragons.

Without warning, Goldilox started playing her Secret Trumpet super loud!

The dragons woke up, saw the Knight, and attacked! (Dragons hate Knights.) They leapt at him, teeth biting, claws clawing, and horns horning.

The Knight had been taken completely by surprise. He fought as best as he could, which wasn't very well at all. Goldilox had told him he was going to be performing sword juggling tricks at her nephew's birthday party, so he hadn't even brought his extra sharp sword.

The Knight was actually allergic to dragons, so he sneezed and got boogers all down the inside of his helmet. Gross!

Meanwhile, Goldilox used the distraction to sneak inside the cave. She filled her bag with acorns, chuckling to herself about how clever she was.

Henry, the dragon with the best hearing (and also the best posture), heard this clever-chuckling and spotted the intruder.

He roared a mighty firey roar, cooking a pile of nearby acorns, which popped like popcorn.

Goldilox acted quickly, and took off one of her gloves. She reached out her hand and touched the fire, turning it into Solid Gold!

(Actually, fire isn't a solid, it's energy. So it turned into Un-Solid Gold, and just floated in mid-air, which was extra cool.)

8

The dragons were so impressed, they just gave Goldilox all the acorns, and in exchange, she turned more stuff into gold for them. Dragons like gold waaaaay more than dumb ol' acorns.

They even helped load the stolen acorns into their van and delivered them to the King of the Squirrel's Castle. How thoughtful!

The Squirrel King ended up falling in love with SoulCruncher. They had little hybrid squirrel-dragon children, which were both cute and freaky looking at the same time.

The knight (who's name I never actually mentioned) stayed eaten. Kinda sad, I know, but he was actually a pretty grouch once you got to know him, so he probably deserved it.

THE END.

The moral of this story is: DON'T. Don't do anything that Goldilox did, she's a terrible role model.

the CiNDERELLA-TRON 5000

illustrated by Jake Standley

The Happy-Smiley-Number-One Robot Corporation designed and manufactured robots.

Chess-Playing-Robots, Bubble-Gum-Chewing-Robots, Punching-Robots, all kinds. House-Cleaning-Robots were their most popular. The Butler-tron 4000 was top of the line, it could vacuum your laundry, cook your dinner, and paint your house, all at the same time. It would even wash your hair and tie your shoes for you if you were feeling especially lazy (and it's amazing how lazy you can feel when you own a Butler-tron 4000).

The Company employed Three Chief Scientists. Filbert was the Smartest Scientist, Cranbert was the Strongest Scientist, and Danklebert was the Craziest Scientist.

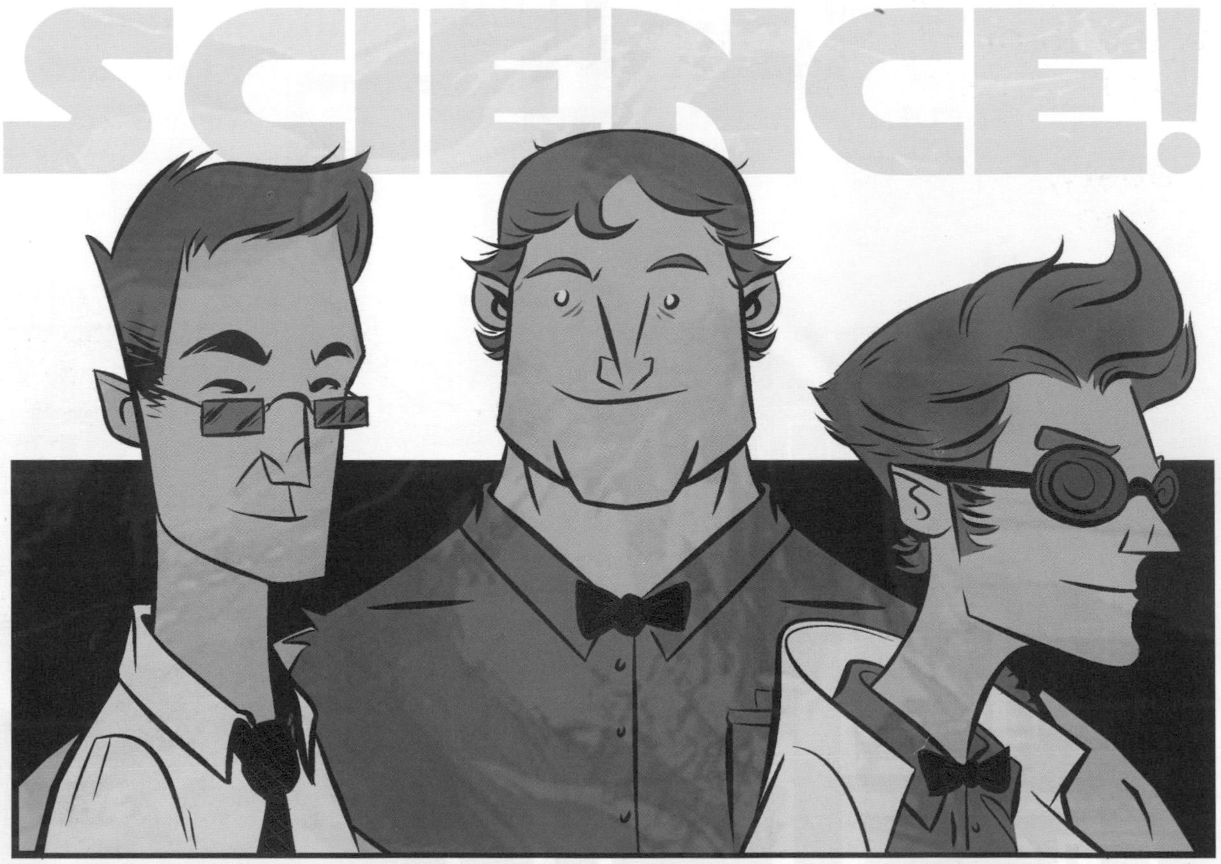
SCIENCE!

They designed shiney new upgraded versions of the Butler-tron. After months of work, they were ready to unveil the new prototype. It was called the Cinderella-tron 5000.

Why? Well, when Danklebert was filling out the patent application paperwork, he had his fingers on the wrong buttons of his keyboard, so instead of typing 'B' he hit 'C', instead of 'U' he typied 'I', etcetera.

THIS IS THE ONLY REASON.

They decided to test the experimental Cinderella-tron 5000 in the dirtiest house in the world, which was owned by the Three Dirty-Little-Gross-Disgusting Pigs.

The pigs had made their house beyond messy. It was full of all the worst things you can think of, and more.

Seriously, don't go in there.

The Scientists had tested all their robots at this house.

The Butler-tron 1000 had exploded before it set foot through the door.

The Butler-tron 2000 had made it inside, but rusted before it could even start cleaning.

The Butler-tron 3000 cleaned for twelve minutes, before bursting into tears and crying for its mommy.

(The Scientists very kindly built it a mommy so it would stop blubbering).

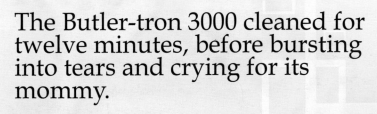

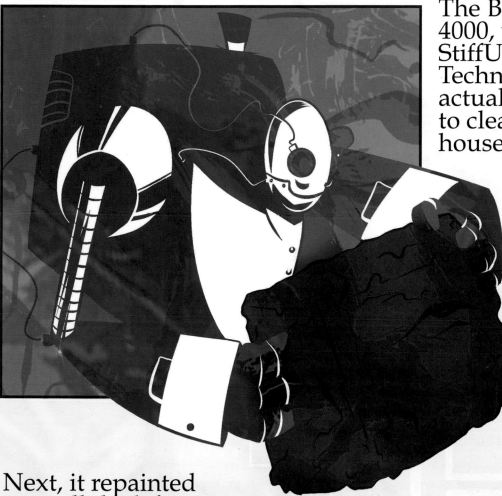

The Butler-tron 4000, with patented StiffUpperLip™ Technology actually managed to clean most of the house!

First it compacted all the sludge into a giant cube, then it hurled the sludge cube into space.

Next, it repainted over all the leftover gunk, trashed all the dead mice, and sprayed the whole place with Air-Freshulizer.

It did a pretty good job! The only problem was that it had taken it seven years to complete that job.

That's just too many years.

The scientists were hoping the Cinderella-tron 5000 could do it in half that time.

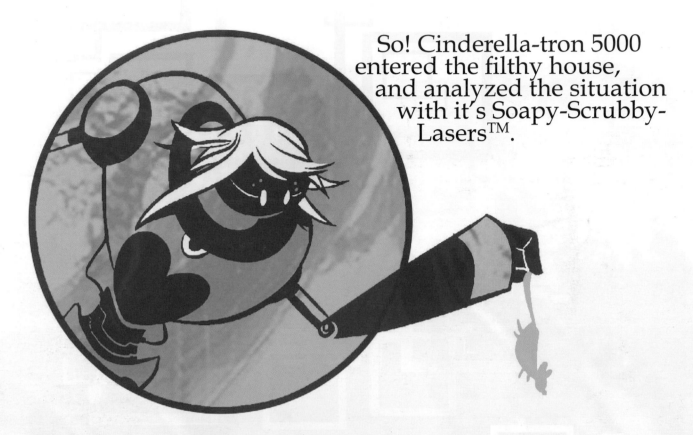

So! Cinderella-tron 5000 entered the filthy house, and analyzed the situation with it's Soapy-Scrubby-Lasers™.

It calculated that it would be easier to demolish the entire house, then rebuild it exactly the same only without any dirt. (This counts as cleaning according to The Rules.)

The Scientists jumped for joy, and had a celebratory luau at their time-share condominium in Hawaii.

The Happy-Smiley-Number-One Robot Corporation ordered the factory to start churning out hundreds of Cinderella-tron 5000s.

The Butler-tron 1000-4000 stepsister robots weren't very happy, but they kept quiet about it, because that was how they had been programmed.

The Three Dirty-Little-Gross-Disgusting-Smelly Pigs were upset, but nobody cared what they thought, because pigs always have dumb opinions.

And then, tragedy struck.

Danklebert had hidden the blueprints in his shoe while he went swimming. At 5 o'clock, when the ocean closed, he toweled off, and found that his shoe was missing! Was it Corporate Espionage, the tide, or just forgetfulness? Nobody knew! And nobody could build Cinderella-trons without those blueprints either. Dang!

After a bunch of meetings and shouting, The Happy-Smiley-Number-One Robot Corporation declared customers could now RENT The Cinderella-tron 5000 Prototype for a million dollars per hour. Totally worth it if your mansion is dirty, am I right? I am right.

THE END.

The moral of this story is: Keep an eye on your shoes dummy!

Hansel
and
Gretel
and
Zorbax

Illustrated by
Michael Spiers

You've heard the story of Hansel and Gretel before, right?

Some demented children get lost in the woods, blah blah blah, leave a trail of breadcrumbs for some reason, find a witch minding her own business, do nasty things to her, the end.

WELL.

The first thing you have to realize, is that Hansel and Gretel are actually space aliens from the Garbonzo Galaxy.

Without that piece of information, the story doesn't make any sense.

Yes, Hnzl and Grtl were the advance-scouts for the Garbonzo Armada.
They came to Earth to test how tasty the planet was.

The Garbonzonites are an alien species that eats EVERYTHING. Rocks, Trees, Bugs, Oxygen, even Broccoli.

They send out scouts to all kindsa planets, and if they think the planet tastes good, they'll activate their BRD-CRM tracking beacon, and an armada of PIK-NIK Battle Cruisers will arrive. Then the Garbonzonites will eat and eat and eat, breakfast, lunch and dinner, until all that's left is the planet's molten core, (which no one likes because it's too spicy).

So, Hnzl and Grtl were gnawing their way through a forest, when they came upon a giant pile of gingerbread, that sorta looked like a cottage if you squinted. Gingerbread tastes waaay better than raw trees, it doesn't matter which galaxy you're from.

This is where Zorbax comes into the story. She is the Witch, or actually, a Widj, from the planet Widjet-7.

Her home planet had been eaten by the Garbonzonites. She had come home from space-vacation to find that her home, the place where she kept ALL HER STUFF was gone. Eaten. Destroyed.

All that was left was a bunch of used napkins and empty bottles of Garbonzo Cola. She decided to get REVENGE! So she set a trap.

The icing on the giant pile of gingerbread was secretly made of LASERS! When Hnzl and Grtl ate through all the cakey-goodness, they found themselves in a cage made of super-sharp light. You can't eat light, even if you put it in a salad.

Zorbax the Widj did a dance of triumph. Her plan had succeeded perfectly!

Then she realized she hadn't really thought her plan all the way through.

She had no idea what to do next.

21

Suddenly, the Garbonzo Armada arrived!
Hnzl and Grtl had activated their BRD-CRM tracking
beacons! THE EARTH WAS DOOMED!

They parked their space ships, got out their spoons, and
were about to dig in, when BOOM! Meteors rained down
upon them, crushing and exploding EVERYTHING!

You see, all the OTHER aliens who had also had their
planets eaten, teamed up, and came up with a plan that
actually had two parts. First, they built a bunch of rockets
and attached them to asteroids,
THEN they aimed them
at the planet the
Garbonzonites
would devour
next.

Brilliant!

Sadly, the meteors that destroyed the Garbonzo aliens also killed all the dinosaurs.

YES! I said this story takes place on earth, but what I didn't say is that it took place on earth sixty-five million years ago!

Ha! I bet you weren't expecting THAT!

THE END.

The moral of this story is: Dinosaurs were really cool, and if they still existed today, I would totally ride one while wearing a cowboy hat.

Also, try not to destroy other peoples planets.

It's rude.

Little Red Robin Hood

Illustrated by Sonny Liew

Little Red Robin Hood was a bird.

A robin, naturally.

She was not very big, and was a sort of reddish-brownish color.

I'm not sure what the 'hood' part of her name comes from.

Either it's because of that cloak thing she wears, or maybe because she's 'in da hood'. (Like, in a rapping way, with gangsta hand gestures and stuff. Sheesh, I dunno, cut me some slack.)

Little Red Robin Hood robbed from the rich, and gave to her poor grandmother (who was now fantastically rich, richer than all the rich people).

Quite frankly, it was now probably easier to just rob from her grandmother, then give it right back to her grandmother. But that would be weird.

Little Red Robin Hood's nemesis was the Sheriff of Naughtyham (who was secretly a werewolf).

His official police horse had lost its head in a waterskiing accident, so doctors had replaced it with a pumpkin. That's just the sort of thing that happens in this book, don't question it too hard. Probably the horse just didn't have good medical insurance.

The Sheriff had a warrant for Little Red Robin Hood's arrest, because of all that stealing she had been doing. The Sheriff also had an army of zombie lawyers, hired by all the rich people who wanted their riches back.

The Sheriff, his horse, and Zombie Lawyer Number One were driving through the woods one day. Suddenly, Little Red Robin Hood zoomed past, exceeding the speed limit, running a stop sign, and giving the Sheriff a very rude hand gesture indeed.

They chased Little Red Robin Hood through the forest; it was all very exciting and dramatic.

Sadly, car chases don't work very well in books, mostly because there's no way to play loud car-chase music.

(I suppose you can try whistling some chase music, but it just wouldn't be the same).

Racing at top speed, Little Red Robin Hood grabbed a handy vine, and swung up into a tree, Tarzan- style.

(Don't try this at home folks, although feel free to try it in a forest).

The Sheriff and his posse crashed into the tree. Dazed, they tumbled from their vehicle. (the Zombie Lawyer tumbled while looking through the car's glove compartment for the insurance paperwork.)

Suddenly, the full moon came out from behind some clouds! (Yeah, I know it's daytime. The moon can come out whenever it wants. Nobody bosses the moon around). The Sheriff of Naughtyham transformed into a MIGHTY WEREWOLF! AROOOOOOOOOOOOOOOOO!

"My what big teeth you have," observed Little Red Robin Hood.

"My, what silky fur you have.
Do you use conditioner?"
Asked the Headless Horse.

"Rawr. Grr. Arg. Braaaaaaains!"
quipped the Zombie Lawyer.

The werewolf
pounced!

The horse climbed up the tree lickety-quick (horses are natural climbers), but the zombie was too slow- (it was the lurching kind of zombie, not the speedy kind) and so it got eaten. Inside the werewolf's stomach, the zombie lawyer served the Sheriff's spleen with a restraining order.

Little Red Robin Hood and the horse debated what to do. They didn't have any silver bullets. They didn't have any silver arrows. They did have some anti-werewolf spray, but it was in the horse's car, where they couldn't reach it.

What they DID have was Little Red Robin Hood's Motorcycle. So they shoved the bike out of the tree, onto the werewolf's head, pinning him to the ground. Hooray!

The two heroic heroes shook hands in triumph, and then the horse slapped handcuffs on Little Red Robin Hood's wrists. She went to jail, and spent every day lifting weights, getting tattoos, and planning revenge.

Red's Grandma emptied her bank accounts and fled the country. Her current whereabouts are unknown.

The Sheriff attended lycanthropy rehab, and went on to appear in the story '*The Big Rad Wolf vs The Three Dirty-Little-Gross-Disgusting-Pigs.*'

Horse was promoted to Police Commissioner, and eventually ran for President.

The Sun and Moon's epic battle for sky domination rages to this day.

THE END.

The moral of this story is basically the same as Goldilox's.

HUMPTY DUMPTY

and the

BREAKFAST of CHAMPIONS!

Illustrated by JjAR

Humpty Dumpty was a giant weirdo egg-person. Don't ask for any kind of explanation, because you won't get one.

Sorry.

He was named Humpty Dumpty because what else would you name a giant-weirdo egg-person? Veronica?

I don't think so.

Humpty was sitting on a wall one day, like a doofus. Who sits on walls these days? Nobody, that's who.

Thin shelled creatures **definitely** shouldn't. Walls are sharp.

Humpty sliced down the middle, spilling his yolk and albumen all over the alleyway.

(Those are fancy words for *stuff inside eggs*.)

Fortunately, at that EXACT MOMENT, three wandering scientists from a previous story rode into town.

They were looking for their missing shoe.

Charlie, their pumpkin-headed horse had a PhD in glueing.

Together, they patched Humpty Dumpty up and used some science to bring him back to life. They couldn't find his arms or legs, but why would an egg have legs in the first place? IT MAKES NO SENSE!

So they made him some cool robot appendages.

The New and Improved Cyborg Humpty Dumpty was super strong, so he got a job at a pest control company.

There were lots of goblins and ogres infesting the neighborhood, so he would run around, grab them, and throw them off a cliff. This is how you deal with vermin.

Humpty got so good at his job, that the president made him Chief Monster Smasher of the World.

One day, he got a phone call saying that the International Museum of Pancakes was having a crisis!

So, Humpty pressed a special button on his coffee mug, which sent a signal that converted his couch (made of donuts) into a catapult, which launched him KABLAM out through the window and into his waiting helicopter.

The helicopter was made out of bacon.

By the way, eggs are very aerodynamic, and perfect for launching at things.

He flew to the scene, and found it swarming with Toast Ghosts.

Apparently, the museum had been built on an Ancient Marmalade Burial Ground. This ALWAYS causes trouble.

It looked like it was time for the ULTIMATE BREAKFAST SHOWDOWN!

Humpty Dumpty drew back his mighty arm, set his fist to MAXIMUM PUNCHING, and slugged one of the ghosts right in it's ghostly ghost-head. It went right through.

Ghosts are immune to punching. They are also immune to the common cold, and criticism.

Thinking quickly, several hours later, Humpty Dumpty picked up the entire museum, and threw it off a cliff, solving the problem once and for all.

THE END.

The moral of this story is:
Giant Eggs are NOT TO BE TRUSTED.

If you spot one in your neighborhood, please call a special hotline!

the Tortoise and the HAIR

Illustrated by Beth Sleven

The tortoise in this story is usually just called *The Tortoise*, but I think that's dumb.

Tortoise, close your eyes, flip through that phone book there, point to a name, and that's what we'll call you.

Good! What did you pick? *CHOMPY?* That's dumb, too!

Pick again.

No? You like the name Chompy?

FINE.

Chompy the Tortoise was sad.

Sadder than that.

Better.

Chompy was sad because he had no hair.

Yes, tortoises don't usually ever have hair, but this tortoise had accidentally been sent to Mammal Junior High School and all the rabbits and squirrels had laughed at him, damaging his self-esteem.

Chompy flicked through his phone book again, and found an advertisement for *Hand Knitted Woolen Toupees*. He called them, gave them his credit card information, and six to eight weeks later, a box of hair arrived. Hooray!

Chompy put the fake hair on, and walked down the street with his head held high. Too high actually, and the hair slipped right off. Everyone nearby laughed at him, and several people who weren't nearby laughed at him too, which was extra hurtful.

This is the saddest part of the story. We printed this page on extra soft paper, so you can use it as a tissue to blow your nose.

That night, Chompy couldn't sleep very well. He kept having nightmares full of evil combs and demon barbers. So instead, he drank some cold hot-chocolate, and watched the weird infomercials that are always on late night television.

Some guy came on the screen, and began to talk about his *Miracle Elixir with Guaranteed Results** (results not guaranteed). He poured a bottle over his head, and instantly became all fuzzy, and also wuzzy.

"That's right folks! Now I can pretend to be a little bunny rabbit ... just like I always dreamed. Call today, and send us ALL your money!"

1-800-BUY-BYE-BUY

Chompy did, and the very next month, another package arrived in the mail. He wrapped it in wrapping paper, pretended it was a present from a secret admirer, unwrapped it, pretended to be surprised, and poured the bottle over his noggin. Instantly, he grew a fantastic pile of hair!

It was real, therefore, life was wonderful! He spent the next several hours combing it before going for another walk outside.

He paraded down the street a second time, head held as high as humanly possible. Er, tortoisefully possible. This time, everybody gave him compliments and even a round of applause.

The local news team from Channel Six (who had been filming a special report about streets) hired Chompy to be their new Channel Six Action News Anchor.

Chompy got to sit behind a fake desk, smile a fake smile at the camera, and tell people about all the explosions that had happened that day.

It wasn't very fulfilling. He had become the very thing he hated most. (He hated TV news, and always changed the channel when it came on.)

He realized that if nobody liked him for his own unique qualities and stuff, they probably weren't worth being friends with in the first place or whatever.

His therapist had been telling him this for years, but he only realized it just now. Epiphanies are like that sometimes.

Chompy quit the news studio, went home, and drank the rest of the bottle of Miracle Elixir. He grew enormous piles of hair all over his body, and he also grew to be 87 feet tall. (That's one of the side effects. It says For External Use Only right there on the bottle. Sheesh.)

He went back to the street, and started crushing buildings and throwing cars around. Everyone who had been mean to him earlier (who apparently had nothing better to do than hang around the same street all day) panicked in fear. Channel 6 news reported that a Yeti was attacking the down-town area.

Chompy had never felt happier.

He probably needs more therapy.

THE END.

The moral of this story is: Don't be mean to people who are different than you, OR ELSE!

The EMPEROR'S NEW NOSE

Illustrated by
Ernst Heijn

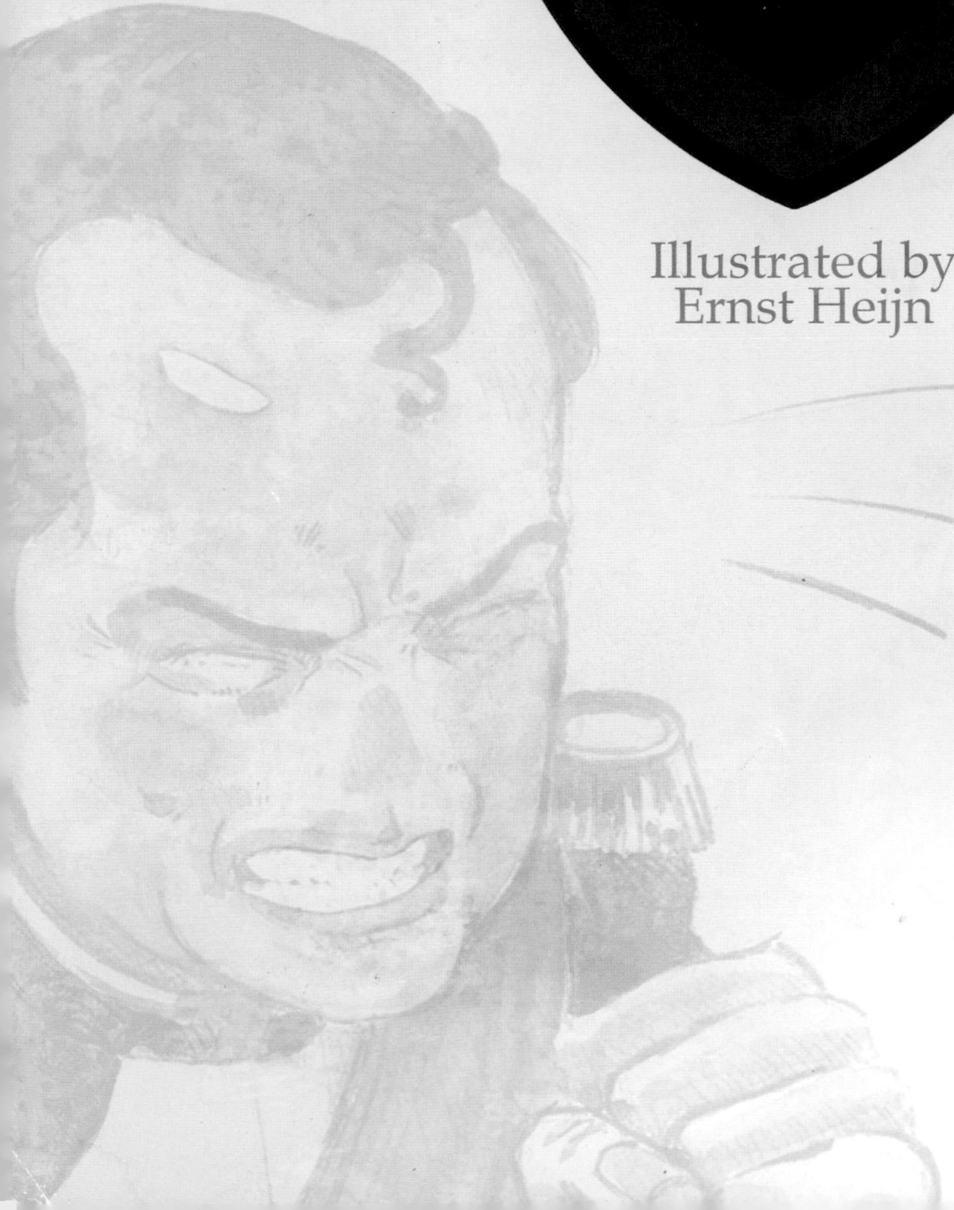

The Emperor of Potato Island was having a birthday party. It wasn't his birthday or anything, he just wanted some attention. And cake. Nobody says no to your crazy requests when you're the Emperor.

He sent out invitations to the King of Squirrels and President Horsepumpkin.

They RSVP'd "Maybe."

The problem was, The Emperor was terriblyworried about thieves stealing all his birthday presents.

Word on the street was that Goldilox had busted Little Red Robin Hood out of jail, and they had teamed up with Ali-Baba and his 40 Convicted Felons to perform some spectacular heists.

The Emperor called his three chief magicians into the room, and filled them in on these startling developments.

Filbert was the Wisest Magician, Cranbert was the Magician with the Best Haircut, and Danklebert was the Magician with the Most Action-Figures (and he would let you play with them if you asked nicely).

The Emperor asked if they would invent him (magically) some sort of something, that would let him turn everything he owned invisible. Thieves can't steal what they can't see after all (and you can look that up in the dictionary if you don't believe me).

The Magicians toiled all night in their laboratory, stopping only to check their email. They soon realized that turning stuff invisible is really hard. So instead, they invented a Molecular Dissolver Fluid. If you spray it on stuff, that stuff completely disappears - as in, no longer exists, PERMANENTLY AND FOREVER.

They told the Emperor that yes indeed, their invention makes stuff disappear, just like how he asked, golly-gee. They had their fingers crossed the whole time, however.

Holding the spray can the wrong way, the Emperor spritzed himself in the face, dissolving his nose so fast it didn't even hurt. There wasn't any blood, because this is a children's book.

The Three ~~Scientists~~ Magicians had TRICKED HIM. His nose was gone forever. He totally fell for it though, and so he pranced around his whole palace, spraying everything until he ran out of spray.

"How do I make stuff reappear?" he asked. "I want my nose back now."

The Emperor loved his nose, and would pick it every day.

He even still had the trophy from his third grade smelling bee in his trophy case. (Actually he didn't; he had sprayed his trophy case with dissolving spray. But he THOUGHT he still had it. Get it?)

The Scientists used big words and techno-jargon to explain how his nose could never return, but made it sound as if this wasn't their fault.

After throwing a tantrum and making a few prank phone calls, the Emperor demanded that they invent him another thing that could magically transpose other people's noses onto his face, so he could borrow the loveliest nose in the world from whoever owned the loveliest nose in the word.

The Scientists shrugged, and got to work.

They built such a device out of rocks and twigs (All their lab equipment had been made "invisible" too, which registered an 8.7 on the Karma-Meter in Danklebert's pocket).

Their Nose-Borrow-o-tron 5000 device didn't actually work, but it had a lightning bolt drawn on it, so it looked really high-tech.

The Emperor fired the Nose-Borrow-o-tron 5000, and Cranbert quickly taped a potato onto his face, tricking him once again. They all told him how handsome and distinguished he looked, while trying not to giggle.

He gave them each half his kingdom as a reward.

Emperors can't do math very well.

THE END.

The moral of this story is: Telling lies can get you both IN and OUT of trouble, so make sure you practice lying so you get really good at it.

THE Fugly DUCKLING

Illustrated by
Phillip Blackman

The North American Fugly Duck (Latin Name: *Anatidae fuglicus*) is a species that went extinct thousands of years ago, and for a good reason too: It was just too *flippin' ugly* to survive.

However, the Three Scientists (who have already appeared in this book waaaaaaay too often) found one frozen in a glacier.

After extracting its DNA, they cloned it back to life. Cloning is super-easy!

It was hatched and raised by a mother Moose Goose, its closest living relative.

They all got along just fine.

THE END.

This story doesn't have a moral. Deal with it.

The Complete Works of

William Shakespeare

by

Charles Dickens

Illustrated by
Roger Langridge

Once upon a time in the year 1597, Romeo and Juliet were two star-crossed lovers. I prefer to keep my stars perpendicular rather than crossed, but I'm modern and hip like that. Also, I don't have big poofy sleeves.

Romeo and Juliet loved each other so much that they accidentally became dead, it was all very poetical and romantic, I'm sure you'll understand when you're older.

Police Commissioner Hamlet (who was not a talking pig even though he had a perfect talking pig kinda name) suspected there was foul play.

So he made a phone call to his golfing buddy, Sherlock Holmes, who agreed to travel back in time and help solve the mystery.

Worried that people would wonder what exactly London's most famous consulting detective would be doing in fair Verona where we lay our scene, Sherlock Holmes decided to wear a disguise.

After much knitting and swearing, he emerged from the sewing parlor dressed as **Dreadlock Holmes, Rastafarian Detective**. Sherlock is kinda dumb in this adaptation. Doctor Watson dressed up as **Doctor Flotsam** by wrapping an electric eel and some seaweed around his head. Watson is dumb pretty much always.

That's right Sir Arthur Conan Doyle! I'm messing up all your characters! AHAHAHAHAHAH! Ahem.

So, after squinting through a magnifying glass, and saying "AHA!" a bunch, Sherlock declared that it WAS murder.

MURDER MOST FOUL.

Romeo and Juliet were brought back to life, by using the power of love and truth, hope and justice, dark science, and just a smidge of voodoo. They were found guilty of homicide, and executed. Their deaths were much less poetic and romantical this time.

Actually, that's awful! I don't know how I let myself get away with such shoddy storytelling! Let's say they came back to life again as zombies. Smooching zombies. Yeah! That's better.

Speaking of which, later that night, Ebeneezer Scrooge was visited by seventeen ghosts, who performed an elaborate musical number about what a horrible person they thought he was.

Doctor Flotsam ate an entire bubble gum pie all by himself and got a tummy ache. Dreadlock Holmes and Police Comissioner Hamlet realized that neither one of them were from fairy tales, and had no business being in this ridiculous book, so they escaped.

THE END.

The Moral of this story is a Secret Mystery. Follow the Clues and figure it out your own self!

SNOW WHITE and the SEVEN DORKS

Illustrated by
Rich Koslowski

Snow White worked at a Technical Support Center. People would call her when they had broken their computers and she would try not to roll her eyes.

She had six clients who were especially dorky and called her all the time:

Snappy, Flappy, Trappy, Clappy, Frappé, and Hank.

Snappy
had spilled
coffee on his
keyboard.

Flappy
had
downloaded
a virus.

Trappy
had frozen
his monitor--
In a block of
ice.

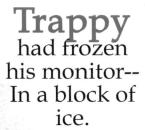

Clappy
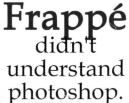
had a real
live mouse
instead of
the kind you
point and
click.

Frappé

didn't
understand
photoshop.

Hank
had tossed
his whole
computer
off a really
tall
building.

Here's the secret you probably guessed: All these dudes had injured their computer on purpose, in order to to speak with Snow White, whom they all had a pretty big crush on.

The secret you probably didn't guess is that all these dudes were actually part of the same giant seven-headed monster-creature-thing!

They all shared the same computer.

It was the most damaged computer in all the land.

If you used your counting, you'll see that there was a seventh head named Mappy-Bo-Bappy, who was actually a cool guy. He was NOT into Snow White, like, at all. He thought she had a weird name, and her personality seemed to consist entirely of eyeball rolling.

"You guys don't even know what she looks like!" he'd yell when he just wanted to check his dang email, and all his fellow heads were thinking of new ways to fragment their hard drive.

"She SOUNDS pretty!" they all replied in unison. It was creepy.

And so, the six dorky heads decided to have a punching contest, the winner would work up the nerve to ask Snow White out on a date.

It did not end well.

The heads all got amnesia from too many blows to the head, and completely forgot Snow White's Technical Support Hotline Phone Number.

They never called her again.

This ending is actually double sad, because it turns out Snow White was ALSO a seven headed monster creature thing!

They had so much in common!

Snow White and her sister-heads eventually got promoted to Assistant Manager, and used their

extra salary to invest in a trendy fried-coffee franchise.

THE END.

The moral of this story is: Dating is awkward!
Especially if you're a seven-headed monster-creature.

You just gotta get yourself out there!
Go to parties, meet new people, maybe try online dating?
But remember, always be yourself. But also be extra charming.

A box of chocolate flowers certainly couldn't hurt,
and brush your dang teeth once in a while!

THE
MICROSCOPIC
MERMAID

IlluClayted by Christi Friesen

Sailors have long believed that the sea is full of mermaids.

Y'know, saucy, beauteous fish-ladies, who quite enjoy the company of grizzled squinty men with anchors tattooed on their arms. Sailors are lonely.

But they're also right, because the sea is FULL of mermaids! They're just not human sized ...

Take a drop full of sea water, and put it under a microscope (send seven proofs of purchase to the Science Crunchies Cereal Corporation if you don't have your own microscope). If you look closely, at magnification 50X, you'll see all kinds of crazy bacteria, microbes, plankton and even a couple mermaids. Yup, they're itty-bitty teeny-tiny, but they do exist, and they are very saucy indeed!

50X MAGNIFICATION

The tiniest and loveliest of all the mermaids was named Aerial. This was because of the antennae she had sticking out of her head so she could pick up radio signals better, and blast out some danceable tunes for her glob-fish friends.

The eyeball looking through the microscope lens belongs to Cranbert, the Most Lovey-Dovey of the Three Scientists Who All Shared The Same Microscope. (Filbert was the most Rational and Platonic Scientist, and Danklebert was the Scientist Who Stayed Out Way Too Late Partying Most Weekends, Even When He Had Important Stuff To Do On Monday.)

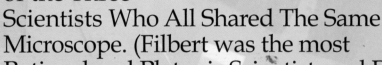

As he ate his Science Crunchies (Now with Electron-Shaped Marshmallows!) Cranbert realized he was madly in love with The Microscopic Mermaid.

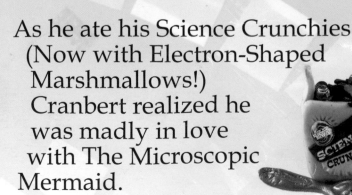

You're probably thinking that the characters in this book fall in love WAAAAY too quickly. Well, I'm not writing a romance novel here people, full of smooches and long smoldering glances. Okay, FINE, you can have ONE smoldering glance, BUT THAT'S IT. Now back to the story.

Cranbert decided to use his experimental Enlarge-o-Ray to make Aerial human sized. This was the same Growth Ray he had used to turn Chicken Little into Chicken Huge, in a story that ended up getting cut out of this book.

ARTIST'S IMPRESSION

Cranbert hit the Enlarge-o-Ray switch. Filbert and Danklebert pedaled the electricity generating bicycle they used when they didn't feel like paying their overdue electric bills.

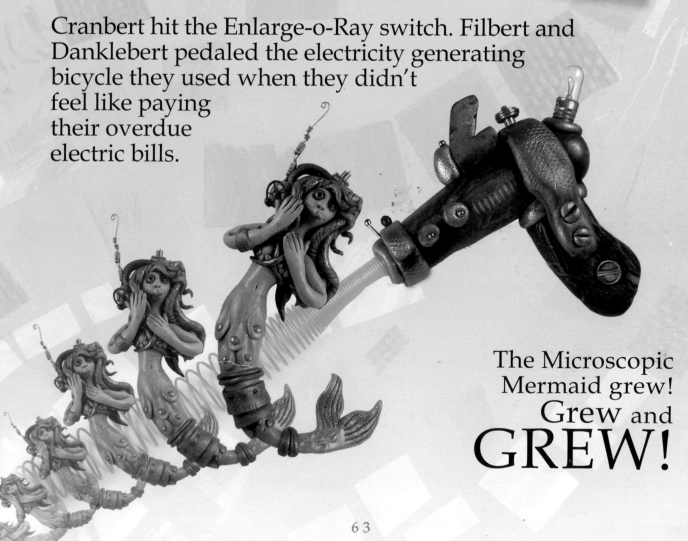

The Microscopic Mermaid grew! Grew and GREW!

Larger and larger Aerial expanded, until finally she was six inches taller than Cranbert! This was actually slightly too tall for his tastes, and he wished he had shut the machine off a second earlier.

After a brief smoldering glance, Aerial fell head over heels in love right back at Cranbert, despite the fact she didn't have any heels. They were very happy together, until they realized they were actually very sad.

Being essentially an enormous one-celled organism, Aerial found that the force of gravity was too strong for her new size. She could barely move, let alone boogie. Also she missed her friends the glob fish, whose individual names she couldn't quite remember at the moment.

It's Harold.

So, the science-friends pedaled the electro-bike backwards, sending anti-electricity into the Enlarge-o-Ray, shrinking Aerial and Cranbert back down to itty-bitty teeny-tiny size. This is how science works.

The two were very happy together, especially now that Cranbert didn't have to repay his student-loan bills, since he was too tiny for his creditors to ever find.

The other scientists eventually found love too, sorta. Danklebert started hanging out with a confident, outgoing head named Mappy Bo-Bappy, with whom he had a similar taste in bow-ties.

Filbert stayed single (He was far too busy for any of that mushy human-interaction stuff). However, he did end up building some robotic grandchildren, so his mother would stop nagging him.

They all lived 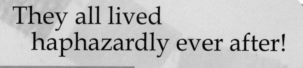 haphazardly ever after!

THE END.

The moral of this story is: Science doesn't solve all your problems. But then again, love never landed on the moon or cured any diseases. You have to combine love and science together if you ever want to get anywhere in this world. Another good combination is Peanut Butter and Chocolate! You should try it sometime.

The
PRINCESS
and the
WHATEVER

Illustrated by

Ian Boothby
Ken Cook
Kit Fox
Asch Kapowi
Timo Kokkila
Batton Lash
Trevin Massey
Scott Meyer
Pete Michels
Scott Christian Sava
Mike Scrase
Michael Spiers
Jesse Smart Smiley
Karen Weiss
Shannon Wheeler
Louis Wilkins

Princess Princessington was the Princessiest Princess in all of Princesslyvania.

And so were all of the other Princesses.

This was because of a mistake at the Princess Factory.

The Happy Smiley Number One Princess Corporation designed and manufactured all kinds of Princesses.

Human Princesses. Penguin Princesses. Rainbow Princesses. Monochromatic Princesses. Pirate Princesses. Ninja Princesses. Space Princesses. Tiny Baby Princesses. Oversized Novelty Princesesses. Detective Princesses. Robot Princesses. Evil Princesses. Quiet Princesses. Loud Princesses. Beefy Princesses. Vegan Princesses. Dainty Princesses. Burpy Princesses.

Princesses for kissing frogs. Princesses for locking in towers. Princesses for Cryogenic Sleep-Freezing. Princesses that find furniture uncomfortable because of vegetables ...

That's just one page of their catalog. You get the idea.

One day, Princess-Technician Sniffany Swink was working the controls of the Princess-o-tron 5000, when she decided to see what would happen if she pressed all the buttons at once.

Well, what ultimately happened was that Sniffany was fired, and a horde of ravenous zombie lawyers (and one peckish zombie paralegal) had to stay up all night filling out boring paperwork to make sure that this sort of thing NEVER HAPPENED AGAIN.

The Happy Smiley Number One Princess Corporation ended up purchasing the now bankrupt Potato Island, and renamed it Princesslyvania.

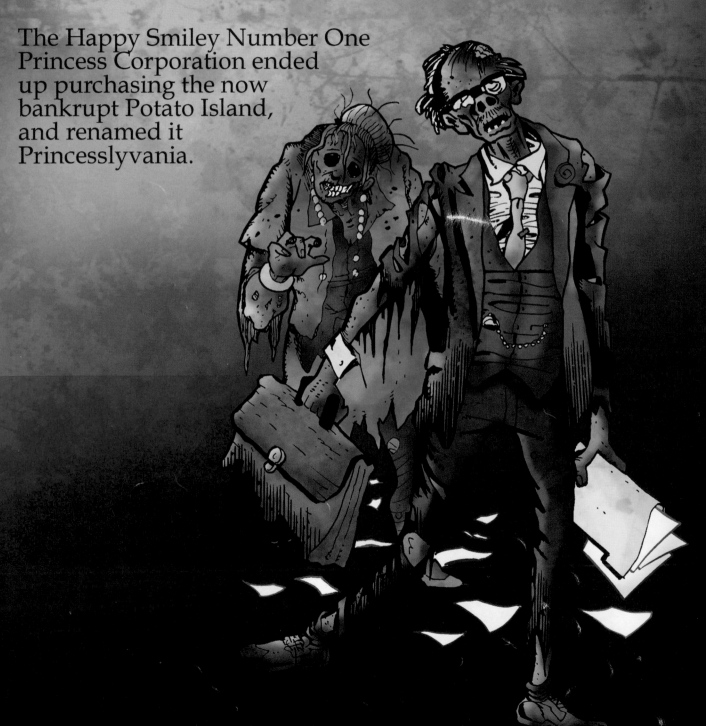

They converted it into a wild princess reserve, where all their surplus princesses could frolic, and have a different crazy princess adventure every single week. I smell a spinoff series!

By the way, this is the last time I'll use the word *Princess* in this book, I promise. I'm sick of hearing it over and over and over and over again too.

THE END.

The moral of this story is: Don't ever make any mistakes.

Author's Outroduction

Photographs by Michelle

Once Upon a Time, at two o'clock in the morning, a cartoonist lurked in his secret fortress, making stuff up, because that was his job.

"What if it turned out, Santa Claus was a Time Traveler? From space? No, that's dumb. Or maybe it's brilliant ..."

"Hey, I know! Maybe the Loch Ness Monster turns out to be Bigfoot in disguise?"

Suddenly, there came a knocking, a knocking upon his chamber door.

Who could it possibly be?

The Pizza Guy?

The cartoonist didn't remember ordering pizza, but then again, he didn't remember NOT ordering pizza ...

Throwing wide the door, he beheld an angry mob of fairy tale characters! The Dinosaur Fairy Princess was disappointed she never had any lines of dialogue. The Three Scientists wanted more money for all their cameo appearances. Little Red Robin Hood wanted revenge for being thrown in jail, when her story could just as easily been written completely differently!

Other characters were mad too about different things.

The cartoonist leapt for his magical reality-changing keyboard, desperately trying to change the ending. Maybe his characters showed up at his house for a tea party, instead of to attack him?

NOPE! TOO LATE!

While Humpty Dumpty and Cinderellatron 5000 held him down, Goldilox stepped forward, removed one of her gloves, and poked her creator right in his big, ugly nose.

His skin crackled, and with a burst of shiny, he turned to solid gold.

Free from the cartoonist's evil control, the characters decided to raid his fridge and eat all his snacks, since that tea party actually sounded like a pretty good idea.

THE ENDINGEST END.

And now!

A brief-yet-comprehensive guide
to all the fabulously talented and
physically attractive humans who
filled this book with such
pretty pictures.

It's the

ILLUSTRATOR BIOGRAPHY PILE!

Make sure you visit their websites
and buy all their stuff, okay?

Phillip 'Nobby Nobody' Blackman

is England's preeminent Beardy Weirdo. He draws the webcomic *Odd-Fish*, a pun filled series of disadventures starring an octopus named Lovecraft. Phillip also designs numerous fake advertisements for the novels of Welsh author Jasper Fforde. Phillip's primary medium is ballpoint pens, though he also works with paint, pastels, and squid.

www.biro-art.com

Christi Friesen

is a pretty big deal in the Polymer Clay Community. She sculpts and writes books and stuff. She's also the author's mother, but don't worry about that right now.

www.ChristiFriesen.com

Ernst Heijn

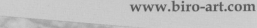

is an illustrator with a background in linguistics and an avid interest in history, archaeology, cacti, and flying things. Ernst lives in Holland for some reason, enjoys the occasional pint of ale, and most dishes containing mushrooms.

www.magpieface.tumblr.com

JjAR

(or Eugene Armenskiy in human language) is a comic artist from Russia. He really is a natural born artist, not because all of his artworks are ingenious, but because drawing for him is a completely natural process ... like eating food, or nose-picking. As well as being way into drawing things, he also is a big video game, animation, and comics maniac.

www.jjar01.deviantart.com

Rich Koslowski

got his "big break" as an artist on the *Sonic The Hedgehog* comic book series in 1993 (yes, he is old) He is best known for his creator-owned series *The 3 Geeks* (later *Geeksville*) and the three graphic novels he had published with Top Shelf Productions: *Three Fingers*, *The King* and *BB Wolf and the Three LPs*. Rich has won numerous ego boosting awards, but still reckons he should have gone into banking and become a real-life super-villain.

www.RichKoslowski.com

Roger Langridge's

works of note include *The Muppet Show Comic Book*, *Thor: The Mighty Avenger*, and a host of others. His self-published series *Fred the Clown* was nominated for a number of Harvey and Eisner awards back when he was young and beautiful. He also created the Eisner Award-winning Lewis Carroll-inspired series, *Snarked!* Langridge lives in London with his wife, his two children, and a box full of his own hair.

www.HotelFred.com

Sonny Liew received Eisner nominations for his art on *Wonderland* (Disney), as well as for spearheading *Liquid City* (Image Comics), a multi-volume comics anthology featuring creators from Southeast Asia. His *Malinky Robot* series was a Xeric grant recipient and winner of the Best Science Fiction Album award at the Utopiales SF Festival. Liew's paintings have been exhibited at the La Luz de Jesus Gallery, Black Earth Museum and the Museum of Contemporary Chinese Art. He lives in Singapore.

www.SonnyLiew.com

Doug Savage draws chickens on sticky notes. No one knows why.

www.SavageChickens.com

Beth Sleven has worked as an animator, character designer, and storyboard artist on a number of projects, including *Looney Tunes: Back in Action*, *Iron Man 2*, and Nickelodeon's *Robot and Monster*. She loves monsters, cheese, and cheesey monster movies. Beth makes fabulous homemade marshmallows; I'm eating some right now. She has a beautiful baby, and a beautiful husband, whose beard is as majestic as a sasquatch in springtime.

www.BethSleven.com

Michael Spiers considers beating 'that-annoying-kid-who-poked-everyone-with-a-pencil' during a junior art competition as a major turning point in his life. Michael has worked for design agencies, sign companies and apparel studios, and has been lucky to illustrate several childrens books in the UK. He now lives in Perth, Australia, where he breeds racing koalas, and occassionally still enters junior art competitions, just to see the looks on everyone's faces. I should really make him draw more dinosaurs, he's awesome at that.

www.MikeSpiers.com.au

Jake Standley worked really hard for way too long in various roles in film and advertising. He moved from his native Florida to Portland Oregon to pursue his lifelong dream of making comics. Jake is deeply mysterious, but only on weekends.

www.JakeStandley.com

Ian Boothby is a prolific scriptwriter, who has double-handedly written more issues of *The Simpsons Comics* than anybody else. He is also quite skilled at catching sandwiches tossed into his mouth. Ian always succeeds at being as Canadian as possible under the circumstances.
www.SneakyDragon.com

Kit Fox lives in Hawaii. Lucky! No trip is complete without her advice on shark attacks and those delicious Portugeuse donut thingees. She draws the webcomic *Snap Crackle Pop!* The only webcomic drawn underwater.
www.HomeOfTheSnap .Blogspot.com

Timo Kokkila is the best Finnish cartoonist there is, as far as I know, I haven't actually checked. If any other comic artists in Finland disagree, I encourage you to challenge Timo to hand-to-hand combat. Most of Timo's characters have a farting-based superpower. Classy!
www.saunalahti.fi/tkokkila/

Trevin Massey Is a graphic designer and freelance matador living in the Houston area. He enjoys Wars that take place amongst the Stars, and being descended from royalty.
www.TrevinMassey.com

Pete Michels is a terriffic animation director, having worked on literally thousands of episodes of *The Simpsons*, *Family Guy*, and *Rick and Morty*. He has also worked on a number of proejcts you haven't heard of, because that's just how Hollywood works sometimes.
www.PeteMichels.net

Mike Scrase was sent from the future to destroy us all, at least according to The Prophecy. Mike is from Bristol, in the UK, so for Mike, every day is *Talk Like A Pirate Day*.
www.Adventures OfZip.co.uk

Karen Weiss and I met at that thing that one time. Actually, I don't think she was there. I wasn't there either. Maybe I'm thinking of someone else? I'm confused.
www.karwei.deviantart.com

Kendraw Cook
I'm pretty sure Kend went to High School with me. I'll prove it: where's my dang yearbook? Ken draws lots of things that are hard to explain. Or are they? Yep. They are.
www.kendraw.tumblr.com

Asch Kapowi is an awesome gender-swapped lieutenant commander Spock cosplayer. If you don't know what any of those words mean, just back away slowly.
www.Melodicmadness .deviantart.com

Batton Lash is the creator of *Supernatural Law*. He also writes the comic *Radioactive Man* (sometimes) *Archie Meets The Punisher* (really!) and lots of other stuff too. He owns every comic book ever published, and will let you come to his house and read them in exchange for a generous tip. You rip it you bought it.
www.ExhibitAPress.com

Scott Meyer owns his own smoking jacket, and consistently takes clipart to the next level. He's written several humorous fantasy novels, and draws a webcomic that is purely an excuse to mock his friend Ric, who had no idea he'd appear in this book wearing a dress, or that it would look so flattering.
www.BasicInstructions.net

Scott Christian Sava
Every time I check this guy's Facebook page he seems to have developed a new talent. Painting, Animationing, Musicing, Movieing, Poeming, Gardening, Hamstering, Comicing, he does everything! LITTERALLY!
www.TheDreamland Chronicles.com

Jesse Smart Smiley is both smart and smiley. His brain and teeth are 150% above the national average. He sleeps during the day, wears lots of capes, and does not show up in mirrors.
www.JesseSmartSmiley. wordpress.com

Shannon Wheeler is the creator of *Too Much Coffee Man*, an occassional contributor to the *New Yorker*, illustrator of *God is Disappointed in You*. Tea is his only weakness, and will cause him to explode.
www.TMCM.com

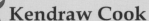

About the Writery Guy

Ray Friesen wrote all of the stories in this book last Thursday, while eating some very inspirational cheese. He illustrated one-and-a-half of the stories, and somehow got a buncha way cool people to draw the rest for him. This was for three reasons: partly for the artistic variety and joy of collaboration, partly to hang all the cool original art on his walls, but mostly for the smug sense of satisfaction in getting people to draw such weird things.

After being turned into gold, bits of Ray were scraped off and made into gold rings and golden teeth. This is a great way to lose weight!

This is Ray's first book without any penguins in it.

www.RayFriesen.com

**THE MORAL
OF THIS BOOK**
is that not all books
are useful or wise.

Some books are just weird
and silly, and hardly
any books have enough
dinosaurs in them. Not
even this one.

THE
END

Now, you can either close
this book and go to bed,
OR
read the whole thing over
again whilst eating
ALL THE COOKIES.

Your choice!